dan zanes

HELLO HELLO

illustrated by
donald saaf

Megan Tingley Books

LITTLE, BROWN AND COMPANY

New York ❧ Boston

to alex, anna, isak, lucian, and olaf

Text copyright © 2004 by Dan Zanes
Hello Hello written by Dan Zanes copyright © 2000 by Sister Barbara Music (ASCAP). Lyrics reproduced by permission.
Illustrations copyright © 2004 by Donald Saaf
Alabama Bound, Crawdad Song, Get on Board Little Children, Mairi's Wedding:
All songs traditional arranged by Dan Zanes
copyright © 2003 by Sister Barbara Music (ASCAP)
℗2003 Festival Five Records, LLC.

Little, Brown and Company

Time Warner Book Group
1271 Avenue of the Americas, New York, NY 10020
Visit our Web site at www.lb-kids.com

First Edition

Library of Congress Cataloging-in-Publication Data

Zanes, Dan.
Hello Hello / by Dan Zanes; illustrated by Donald Saaf.
p.cm.
Summary: An illustrated collection of one original and four traditional songs:
"Hello Hello," "Crawdad Song," "Get on Board Little Children," "Albama Bound," and "Mairi's Wedding."
Includes musical notation.
ISBN 0-316-16808-4
1. Children's songs—Texts. [1. Folk songs.] I. Saaf, Donald, ill. Il. Title.
PZ8.3.Z325He 2004
782.42164'0268—dc21
[E]
2003047446
10 9 8 7 6 5 4 3 2 1

TWP

Printed in Singapore

The illustrations for this book were done using collage, acrylic gouache, flashe paint, and colored pencils on Fabriano paper.
The text was set in Franklin Gothic and Adobe Caslon with woodtype dropcaps.
This book was printed on Cyclus offset produced from 100% recycled fibers with 50% post-consumer waste
and 40% post-industrial waste using a chlorine-free bleaching process.

Designed by Yolanda Cuomo Design, NYC
Associate Designer: Kristi Norgaard

So many things can happen to a song. for example, although i say that i wrote "hello hello," when i really think back to that particular day it seems more accurate to say that it fell out of the sky and landed in my lap. i liked it right away. it was easy to sing and play (and teach someone else), and it said what i was feeling at that moment about friends and neighbors. there did, however, seem to be something missing. i thought for a few days and it finally hit me—it needed some more hellos . . . in other languages.

brooklyn, new yorkio (as woody guthrie called it), is a little world unto itself and it seems that everyone from around the globe is here. i only had to walk a few blocks over to court street to start rounding up my new words. polish, french, spanish, arabic, chinese, hebrew, japanese, everywhere i went people were happy to teach me their greetings and quite interested to hear that they were going to appear in a song.

"hello hello" started to take on a life of its own when i added the various languages at the end. all of a sudden it really was about my neighborhood and the different people that make it such an interesting place to live.

another kind of change happened when my brother-in-law donald saaf took the words and added his beautiful and humorous pictures to them. i didn't realize when i wrote "hello hello" that every inch of wall space in donald's vermont studio would someday be covered with sketches and paintings for this book. the sentiments of the song took on a whole new meaning when i saw the characters walking (and dancing and hopping) through the pages.

there is still another way a song can change, and that's when someone learns it and makes it their own. i always hope when i play a tune that i'm passing it along to somebody else and that they'll use it for a while, anytime people are sitting on stoops, walking to school, picnicking, waiting in line, gardening, running errands, or riding in a car, it's a good time for a song. always have one up your sleeve!

with that in mind, here is "hello hello" with words, music, and donald's paintings. in addition, i've included a cd, which also has four of my favorite folk songs and the lyrics and chords that might help you make them your own. i hope that when you go out into the world, you have a head full of funny pictures and a heart full of songs to sing.

Love, Dan

very day brings more

than the day before

Open any door and say hello
hello
hello

It's the same bright sun shines on everyone

And though the clouds may come
just say hello hello hello

every day is new, so wondrous and few

and a friend comes wandering through
and says hello hello hello

i spy
with my little eye
my shoes grew wings
and learned to fly

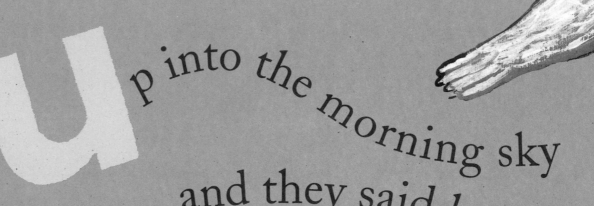

Up into the morning sky
and they said hello hello hello

Hello Hello Hello

HELLO HELLO

one of my favorite things in the world is walking my daughter to school in the morning. we see everybody. we wave hello. it's the greatest way to start the day. here in brooklyn, there are people from all over the world. on any given day we'll hear several different languages being spoken. the street scene in this book shows characters saying hello in sixteen different languages.

italian (italy) ciao
spanish (america, mexico, spain) hola
arabic (north africa, middle east) salaam
english (america, england) hello
japanese (japan) konnichiwa
french (france, belgium) bonjour
hindi (india) namaste
portuguese (portugal, brazil) olá
wolof (west africa) jama ngaam

afrikaans, danish, dutch, german, norwegian, gaelic hallo
hebrew (israel, turkey) shalom
mandarin (china) ni hao
polish (poland) czesc
navajo (america) yá'át'ééh
maori (new zealand) tena koe
kituba (congo) mbote

there are a lot of dogs in our neighborhood too. i don't know what their language is called, but if you look closely, you'll see a greeting.

every day brings more
than the day before

open any door
and say hello hello hello

it's the same bright sun
shines on everyone

and though the clouds may come
just say hello hello hello

every day is new
so wondrous and few

and a friend comes wandering through
and says hello hello hello

i spy with my little eye
my shoes grew wings and learned to fly

up into the morning sky
and they said hello hello hello

hello hello hello

ET ON BOARD LITTLE CHILDREN

i like songs with a positive message that can be learned quickly. when sing-along time rolls around, it helps to have several of these within reach.

one of the exciting things about folk music is the way it changes over the years to meet the needs and desires of the people singing. this song is from the african-american gospel tradition, and during the civil rights era many gospel lyrics were changed to address the issues of the times. i have a recording of the freedom singers doing this one and instead of "there's room for many a-more" at the end of the chorus they sing, "stand up for human rights."

my daughter used to think that i had an imaginary friend named gusto because whenever it came time to really belt it out i would always say, "let's sing this one with gusto!" "get on board little children" is the perfect song for that approach.

the gospel train's a-comin';
 i hear it just at hand.
i hear the wheels a-rumblin'
and rollin' through the land.

get on board little children;
 get on board.
get on board little children;
there's room for many a-more.

i hear that train a-comin';
she's comin' round the curve.
she's loosened all her steam
 and brakes
and strainin' ev'ry nerve.

 get on board…

the fare is cheap and all can go;
 the rich and poor are there.
no second class aboard this train;
 no difference in the fare.

 get on board…

mAIRI'S WEDDING

this song was originally written in the gaelic language of scotland. it's also known as the lawson wedding song. a few definitions may be helpful:

myrtle: a green shrub
bracken: a brown fern
sheiling: a summer pasture in the mountains
peat: partially decomposed and carbonized mosses; often burned for heat
creel: a wicker basket
bairns: children, of course
rowans: the red fall berries of an ash tree

i think of the lyrics to this song as being quite poetic, and yet the melody is so strong that it's often played instrumentally as a dance tune without any singing at all.

Mairi's Wedding

step it gaily off we go- heel for heel and toe for toe-

arm in arm and off we go— all for Mai-ri's wed-ding

O-ver hill-ways up and down— Myrtle green and bracken brown

Past the sheiling through the town all for the sake of Mairi

step me gaily, off we go,
heel for heel and toe for toe,
arm in arm and off we go,
all for mairi's wedding.

over hillways up and down,
myrtle green and bracken brown,
past the sheiling through the town,
all for sake of mairi.

step me gaily...

plenty herring, plenty meal,
plenty peat to fill her creel,
plenty bonny bairns as weel,
that's the toast for mairi.

step me gaily...

cheeks as bright as rowans are,
brighter far than any star,
fairest o' them all by far,
is my darlin' mairi.

step me gaily...

ALABAMA BOUND

music can really open my eyes to the rest of the world. i started thinking about life on the early steamboats when i heard this song recently. men known as roustabouts would be on the docks loading and unloading enormous amounts of cotton among other things from the boats. singing, as it usually does, made the hours more bearable for the roustabouts, and this was one of their tunes. there are also many versions of this song that have been sung by railroad workers.

all over the world people have been singing while they work, play, pray, walk, and do any number of other everyday activities. i'm trying to weave more songs into my daily life. the first step is to learn them!

oh the boat's up the river,
going 'round and 'round,
and the people on the other shore
yell, she's alabama bound!

you want to be like me,
you want to be like me,
you got a friend in birmingham town
and one in tennessee.

doctor cook's in town
he found the north pole so doggone cold,
he's alabama bound!

you want to be like me…

where were you, sweet mama,
when the boats came around?
oh, i was on the other shore
showin' a friend around.

you want to be like me…

now the boat's up the river,
turning 'round and 'round,
and the people on the other shore
yell, she's alabama bound!

you want to be like me…

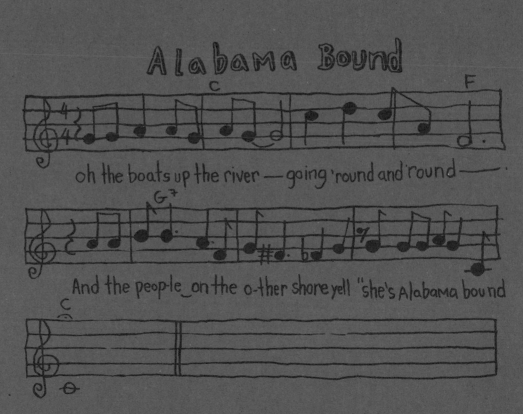

Alabama Bound

oh the boats up the river — going 'round and 'round —

And the people on the o-ther shore yell "she's Alabama bound

CRAWDAD SONG

Caround the time that my daughter was born i bought a banjo. i'd never played one before and felt it was time to learn. there were a few dads that i kept running into out on the playground, and eventually the conversation turned to music. as i discovered, cary played guitar and john played upright bass. we started getting together every thursday night when our kids had gone to sleep, and we'd play old-time songs. this was one of the first tunes we learned.

crawdads (or crayfish, crawfish, or spoondads) are the little cousins of the lobster and they don't have much to do with life in new york, but this song is right for almost any occasion and it's easy to find a harmony part to sing.

you get a line, i'll get a pole, honey,
you get a line, i'll get a pole, babe.
you get a line, i'll get a pole,
we'll go down to the crawdad hole,
honey, sugar baby mine.

wake up old man, you slept too late, honey,
wake up old man, you slept too late, babe.
wake up old man, you slept too late,
i ate the last crawdad off your plate,
honey, sugar baby mine.

yonder comes a man with a sack on his back, honey,
yonder comes a man with a sack on his back, babe.
yonder comes a man with a sack on his back,
packin'all the crawdads he can pack,
honey, sugar baby mine.

what you gonna do when the creek runs dry, honey,
what you gonna do when the creek runs dry, babe?
what you gonna do when the creek runs dry,
sit on the bank and watch the crawdad die,
honey, sugar baby mine.